Naughty Doctor

Zoey Zane

Cover Design by Jillian Liota — Blue Moon Creative Studio

Author Logo Design by Tanya Baikie — More Than Words Graphic Design

Editing by Rachelle Anne Wright — R. A. Wright Editing

Proofreading by Dee — Dee's Notes Editing

.

Dedication

For my ride or die.

The greatest thing you'll ever learn
is just to love and be loved in return.

Moulin Rouge

Fair Warning

Naughty Doctor is a doctor/patient story. It's a standalone dark romance. This novella contains graphic language, explicit sexual content, and situations that some readers may find objectionable: dub-con/non-con/CNC, fisting, and allusions to cheating.

Chapter One

Connor

HER LUSCIOUS CURVES LURE me into a fantasy for the second time today. It's the new receptionist's first day, and when she bends down to reach something in the bottom drawer of the filing cabinet to my left, it's all I can do not to pounce on her.

We haven't been introduced yet, but I'm already dreaming about making her mine. I stifle a groan and bring my attention back to Shannon, who's filling me in on my last few patients of the day.

"This one fractured his arm three weeks ago playing rough with his nephews. Unfortunately, they got the best of him. It's healing nicely, so it should be a quick follow-up. Then you have—" She's interrupted by a loud noise.

I turn around and see the new receptionist tangled up in sparkling lights, holding on to the tree for dear life. I chuckle slightly and raise my eyebrow at Shannon. Seeing the lights tangled around her ankle sends a pulse straight to my cock.

"Shit," she mutters, and rushes over to help the woman. They untangle her from the string of lights and set the Christmas tree down, placing the lights on the ground.

"Shannon?" I call out.

"Right." She motions for the woman to follow her, and they walk toward me. "Leigh, meet Dr. Wilson."

Leigh turns to me and reaches out her hand. "Hello, Dr. Wilson. Sorry about that." Her face turns red as she gestures toward the tree.

I take her hand in mine. "Pleasure to meet you. Not to worry—it can take a beating." I wink, and the color on her cheeks deepens. She averts her gaze from mine. Gently, I squeeze her hand before letting go.

"Leigh will be filling in for me while I'm out," Shannon states.

"Of course." I nod, then turn to address Leigh. "I assume Shannon is showing you the ropes?"

She eyes me briefly, then nods. "Oh, yes, sir. She's been a great help today."

"Good." Both women are looking back at the tree so I take the opportunity to look at Leigh. My hungry eyes roam up and down her body, drinking in her curves. I swear I see her shiver under my gaze. "I—" A bell dings in the waiting area, and the phone rings at the front desk.

Shannon hurries to greet the patient, and Leigh sits in the chair to answer the phone. The receptionist area is in front of a wall decorated with paper ornaments saying so-and-so donated to a charity. Garlands laced with tinsel are taped to the wall, and twinkle lights illuminate the front desk.

"Hello, Dr. Wilson's office." Her voice is more confident than it was a minute ago. She cradles the phone between her ear and neck as she types on the keyboard. *Hmm. She catches on quickly.*

Clearing my throat, I pick up the patient file from the incoming folder and glance it over, then tuck it under my arm, walk out from behind the wall, and call for my next patient—Dylan Carter. He walks toward me, and I motion for him to follow. Before I turn away, I notice Leigh staring at me. I meet her bright gaze, and a faint blush appears on her cheeks. She quickly turns away again and fidgets with something on the desk.

"So, how's the arm feeling, Mr. Carter?"

"Much better, thanks, doc! The sling helped." Dylan's quite fit with an athletic build, standing at six feet three inches tall. Still, his nephews give him a run for his money. Not yet teenagers, but they're getting there.

I've known the Carter twins since they were babies. Hell, I was the one to deliver them. Yep, that's me—Doctor Connor Wilson, OBGYN, jack-of-all-trades. It's hard not to have a basic understanding of a majority of medical specialties, given I'm one of the few doctors in town. Crimson is a small town in the middle of nowhere, Kansas. I've delivered most of the younger generation, in addition to seeing their parents as my patients when they were late teenagers.

Once we reach the room, I give Dylan a once-over, looking for other injuries while also examining his arm. "The new x-rays suggest the arm is healing nicely. I'd recommend the sling for another few days if it's still bothering you. After that, just lay off the twins for a little while."

He laughs and holds up his other hand in surrender. "You're the boss."

I scribble my signature on his discharge paper. "Take this to Leigh, the new receptionist, and she'll get you checked out. Have a nice day."

"You too, thanks." Dylan takes the paper from my outstretched hand and walks back toward the front desk.

I grab the next patient file from the incoming folder and return to my office. There's fifteen minutes before my next appointment, the perfect amount of time to catch up on my notes. After I log into my computer and unlock my notes, I bury myself in busywork. Lost in the lines of medical jargon, I don't hear the knocks until a voice rings out.

"Dr. Wilson?" A velvety voice comes through the cracked door, then another knock. I look up as the door opens a little wider and a head peeks in.

Leigh.

Her striking blue eyes meet mine, and the electric pull between us tugs on my heart. "Yes?"

"Your next patient is here."

I glance down at my watch. "Shit. Thank you, Leigh. Please tell them I'll be right out."

"Yes, sir." She nods.

A few clicks later, I sign off the computer and walk into the waiting room. As I call for the next patient, I feel her eyes on me. Doing my best to ignore her stare, I greet my patient and walk them back into an exam room.

Chapter Two

Leigh

ONE WEEK EARLIER...

I walk into the warm building, unwrap my scarf, and shrug off my coat. Running a hand through my hair, I look around Sweet Apples Bakery. It's usually bustling with customers, no open tables in sight. Today is different.

It must be the cold. Crimson doesn't get much snow, but when we do, everyone stays home. It's not quite snowing yet today, however. There are only a few occupied tables, so I snag the one farthest from the door. I place my coat on the back of the chair and look around for Annie.

A second later, she walks into the room carrying a huge stainless-steel thermos. Her eyes widen when she spots me, and she sets the thermos down next to the coffee on the counter before mouthing *one minute* to me. She adds the apple cider label, reaches under the counter for a couple of mugs, and quickly pours the drinks. She loads up a tray, drops three off at a different table, and brings the last one to me.

Annie smiles as she sets the mug down in front of me. "Hi, Leigh. Did it warm up outside by chance?"

"Annie," I say with a smile. "No. If anything, it got colder!" She chuckles and sits down. "It doesn't look busy today."

She sighs. "Not really. But honestly, I welcome the break. With Christmas around the corner, I've been baking cookies nonstop. Thankfully, I prepped everything for the store early. It makes it so much easier."

I wrap my hand around the warm mug, welcoming the sting of heat against my palm. "I bet it's crazy!"

"Oh, speaking of crazy," she says with a laugh, "Shannon's asked me if we know anyone needing a part-time holiday position."

"For?" I blow at the steam before taking a sip, then let out a moan. "God, this is so good."

Annie's eyes sparkle. She knows her homemade apple cider is the best. Aside from water, all I drink for four months of the year is cider. The recipe has been a family tradition for generations. Annie may be the only baker, but they sure know how to drink. Add a little rum and it's utter perfection.

"The doctor's office she works in. She's moving to a part-time position for the next two months because her stepson is coming home. It's a whole thing, but she needs to be home more for him, so they're looking for someone to help out around the office and pick up the slack when she's away, and I thought of you. I suggested it to Shannon and said I'd ask you."

"Oh, that's kind of you, Annie, but I'm not sure . . ."

A customer walks up to the counter, halting our conversation. I bite my tongue before I give her a run-of-the-mill excuse. Although, I briefly wonder why Shannon hasn't said anything to me about it. We've known each other for a few years, but I know she's closer to Annie than me.

"Hold that thought." Annie grabs the tray and walks behind the counter to ring up the customer. "Have a great day!" she calls out after him, walks over to his table to pick up the dirty dishes, then disappears into the back, behind the door she came out of earlier.

As I watch Annie bustle around before returning to my table, I'm going back and forth between needing the extra money or enjoying the quiet time. Currently, I only have a couple of clients to keep me busy. I enjoy the downtime but like to stay busy during the holidays. As a freelance content writer, my schedule tends to be flexible and allows for massive amounts of downtime if I'm ahead of my deadlines. So, a part-time job would actually be helpful. Annie comes back over and sits down again. "You were saying?"

"It sounds wonderful. I'll reach out to Shannon." I smile and pick up my mug, then take a long sip. "I don't know how you do it. This cider is truly amazing."

Her nose crinkles as she grins. "It's a family secret."

"Yeah, yeah, I know." I roll my eyes and chuckle. "Well, I better head out. I'll need something to wear other than yoga pants and T-shirts if I'm working in an office again."

"I hear the boss is strikingly gorgeous." Annie winks and pulls me into a hug. "Good luck, Leigh. It's always so great to see you."

"You too. It feels like it's been ages."

"Around the holidays, it is," she agrees. A bell rings behind us, and Annie turns around and greets the customer. "I'll see you later." She waves and heads back to the counter.

I fumble around in my purse and locate a ten-dollar bill. I tuck it under the empty mug, then wrap the scarf around my neck. Bracing myself for the cold, I slide on my coat, zip it up, and step outside.

I'm not the type of person to shop for clothes. I know what fits, and I know what I like. I'm the type of person to get my Christmas shopping done early, even before Black Friday, because going to the mall is dreadful. Especially in the middle of the day when it's less busy, because it means you're unable to blend into the crowd. I hate it.

My car rumbles to life, throwing cold air in my face. *Let's get this shit over with.*

I pull into my driveway a few hours later, toting four bags full of new clothes and accessories. It's a slight struggle to make it into the house, but I make it inside with all my fingers intact. The cold is fierce out there.

Dropping my purse onto the couch as I go past, I make my way into the kitchen and set the bags on the table. My conversation with Annie rings in my ears as I move through the kitchen, getting ready for dinner.

I'm grateful places with pre-portioned dinners exist. It makes dinner for one much easier to prepare. You never quite get used to the silence.

Some nights, the silence is deafening. On those nights, I open a bottle of my favorite wine and watch some *Law and Order: SVU* reruns. Gruesome, I know. But there's something about watching Olivia Benson take down the bad guys. It puts me in a better mood each time.

I enjoy my dinner at the table tonight and make a quick call to Shannon. We discuss the position and what she needs from me, then decide I'll start on Monday.

Household chores keep me busy for the rest of the night. I've moved clothes from the washer to the dryer, cleaned the kitchen from top to bottom, and removed all the tags from my new clothes, only to find nowhere to hang them up in the closet. My attire of yoga pants and T-shirts threatens to take over my half, and for a second, I debate calling the whole thing off. The more I reorganize my closet, the more it's apparent something needs to change.

Even if the change is only for a couple of months. Just until the holidays are over.

Chapter Three

Leigh

PRESENT DAY...

It's been three hours, and I have yet to meet the elusive Dr. Connor Wilson. He's had back-to-back patients this morning and hasn't even surfaced for a break. I'm lost in thought when a loud, demanding voice catches my attention.

"Shannon, where are my patient files?"

I spin around and trip over something. My leg gives out from under me, and the papers in my hands go flying. "Ahh!" I fumble to catch my balance, but the giant Christmas tree in the lobby falls over. Seconds later, I'm making more of a mess trying to free myself from the string of Christmas lights than I would had I just fallen with the tree.

Shannon rushes over to me and helps me undo my mess. The lights dig into my ankle, and a slight sting from the heat of the bulbs runs through my leg, causing me to gasp. "Are you okay?" She grabs the tree and sets it back on the ground.

"I've been better." I shrug. "Thanks for helping." With her help, we untangle my leg from the lights, and I gently smooth out my skirt. A tingle runs down my spine when I feel a pair of eyes on me.

"No worries," she says. Before she can say anything else, we're interrupted by someone calling her name. She turns to her right, and I follow her gaze to a drop-dead gorgeous man leaning against the counter.

Oh, shit.

"Right. Leigh, meet Dr. Wilson." Shannon gestures to the man, and I approach him, hand outstretched. *Way to make a good first impression.*

"Hello, Dr. Wilson. Sorry about that." Our fingers touch, and the tingling sensation I felt moments ago morphs into a slow burn.

"Pleasure to meet you. Not to worry—it can take a beating," he says, then winks at me. His sparkling green eyes capture my attention, turning the slow burn into a fiery blaze on my cheeks. I quickly look away as he turns the conversation back to Shannon.

While Shannon fills him in on the details of our day, I allow myself another peek at the man before me. My eyes roam up and down his body, and I focus on his facial features, intrigued by the dimple peeking out from under his day-old stubble.

The bell on the front counter dings at the same time as the lights on the phone shine red. "Excuse me." I race off to answer the phone, holding it to my ear with my shoulder. Turning my attention to the caller, I pull up the scheduling program and quickly find the next available appointment.

Thankfully, the learning curve today isn't too bad. Being a freelancer means I know my way around a computer. I use every program the office uses at home, including the scheduler. It seems like I'm a quick learner, and I am, but honestly, I could do this in my sleep. Shannon quickly realizes she doesn't need to be so hands on, so she gives me a list of tasks for the day and leaves me to my own devices.

I stretch my legs out underneath the counter, trying to take some pressure off my poor soles. High heels and I have never been friends. It's all I can do not to take the shoes off and rub my feet.

Five patient calls, four referrals, three medication refills, and a completed task list later, I glance at the clock. It's just past three in the afternoon. I breathe a sigh of relief as I head into the break room to slip off my heels for a moment. Shannon walks in just as I slip them back on. She has her coat hanging over her arm and a purse in her hand.

"Leigh?"

"Yes?"

"Will you please let Dr. Wilson know he's late for his patient? He's in his office. I'm heading out to pick up my stepson. He arrives today."

"Sure thing." I stand up and run a hand through my hair. "Good luck!"

Shannon turns away but stops. "Oh, and closing up is super easy. I've left another small list next to the phone. If you have any questions, call me." She waves and heads out.

Okay, so it's just me now. I can do this. I walk down the hallway to Dr. Wilson's office and knock.

There's no answer.

After knocking again, I crack the door open and peek my head in. "Dr. Wilson?"

"Yes?" He glances up at me.

"Your next patient is here," I say.

"Shit," he mutters after checking his watch. "Thank you, Leigh. Please tell them I'll be right out."

"Yes, sir." I nod and close the door behind me.

After I inform the patient, I gloss over the closing checklist. Simple enough. It's only a few additional tasks outside of cleaning up.

The cleaning process doesn't take long either. Emptying a couple of trash cans, wiping down the counter, spraying Lysol throughout the waiting room, and ensuring all the supplies are locked up. About fifteen minutes later, the patient returns to the front to check out. We make small talk while I schedule her next appointment and print out her reminder. The phone rings as soon as I hand her the paper back.

"Hello, Dr. Wilson's office." The hairs on my arms rise, and I sit up a little straighter. I know he's watching me. I've felt his eyes on me a few times today. He doesn't speak much, but when I see him, his body language intrigues me.

"Oh, yes, ma'am. We open tomorrow at nine a.m." I pause. "Thank you for calling, have a great night." After placing the phone back on the cradle, I face him.

"Is there something I can help you with, Dr. Wilson?" I raise an eyebrow.

His gaze drifts down to my toes and back up to my face, causing me to squirm in my seat. "How was your first day, Leigh? Shannon showing you the ropes okay?"

"Yes, sir," I confirm, smiling at him. I've known Shannon for about a year, but having a friend at a new job is always good. "She's wonderful."

"That's good to hear. You'll be in great hands with her." He returns my smile and leans on the counter. "Great job today. If everything is done, you are free to go. I can lock the doors behind me."

Dr. Wilson reaches an arm around me to grab my car keys, which were sitting behind me on the counter, and he dangles them in front of me. A small laugh escapes when

I reach for them. Then our fingers touch, and the world stops. He doesn't release the keys but instead holds my gaze, flooding my body with heat.

"Leigh," he breathes.

I blink, and he releases the keys. "Thank you."

He starts to walk away, but I stop him. "Pardon me for being forward . . . I can't help but notice you don't wear a ring. Is there someone waiting for you at home?" *Oh my god.* I am not this bold. Not in a million years. Confident, yes, but making the first move? Never. *What am I doing?* "I'm sorry, I don't know what came over me. You don't have to answer." The words tumble out of my mouth, trying to take it all back. Warmth creeps up my neck as the embarrassment takes over. I look away to avoid his scrutiny.

"Ah, it's something like that." His voice is rough, and he smirks at me. Then, tucking a piece of hair behind my ear, he leans in and whispers, "You have a wonderful evening, little mouse."

Little mouse? He walks away, leaving me stunned. *Did I just hit on my boss? And on the first day. What in the sweet fucking hell was that?*

Chapter Four

Connor

Two weeks later...

Images of Leigh plague my thoughts. The way her hair cascades down her back. The way her smile makes any room brighter. Her plump pink lips and the way they turn up when she's lost in thought. Her long legs and how they would feel wrapped around my waist. How her pussy tastes, and how much I want to sink my cock into her. These are not images I should be thinking about. I'm her boss.

She surprised me when she asked about someone special in my life. Over the past two weeks, we've shared moments where something could happen. Sadly, they're fleeting, making me wonder if they're one-sided.

I'm her boss. Nothing should happen between us. Nothing can happen between us.

Still, my gaze lingers on her body longer than a boss's gaze should. My body responds in a way a boss's shouldn't. I know she feels it too, even though she won't say it.

This pull between us. It's electric. Tantalizing.

Her fingers graze my arm when she passes me in the hallway. The glances are flirty, but coupled with a wicked smile, my insides turn into Jell-O. She teases me when she stretches her legs under the counter as if daring me to look. Her clothes cling to her every curve—curves begging to be touched. She rakes her eyes up and down my body, wanting me as much as I crave her.

"Good morning, Dr. Wilson," she greets me. Leigh walks around the counter, sets her purse down, and removes her coat. She's wearing a graphic T-shirt with Christmas lights and white letters that say "Light It Up," paired with skinny jeans and a pair of snow boots. I forgot today's casual Friday.

I shift my position and discreetly adjust the instant hard-on in my pants. "Good morning, Leigh." *I'm her boss.*

She crinkles her nose and flashes me a smile. "It's going to be a good day today. There's something in the air. I can feel it." Cute green Christmas trees hang from her earlobes, reminding me of the mistletoe I have in my office. I make a mental note to stick it in my pocket for later.

"Yes, it will be," I say, and give her a knowing look. She doesn't know yet just how good today will be. With that, I head into my office in the back and bury myself in my notes before patients start arriving.

A few moments later, Leigh knocks on the door.

"Dr. Wilson?"

"Leigh." I motion for her to come in. "What can I do for you?"

"Mrs. Johnson is here for your nine o'clock."

"Got it. I'll be right out." She steps out of the office, but I'm quick behind her.

"Leigh," I breathe.

She turns around, bumping straight into me. "Oops, sorry." I reach out to catch her, wrapping my arm around her waist before she loses her balance. Her gaze meets mine, heating my insides as I read her expression. Cheeks red, breaths heavy. She's not sorry. Not even a little bit.

"You forgot something."

"Oh, did I?" she asks, innocently looking from side to side.

"Up here?" I tease, wiggling the mistletoe above our heads. Leigh lets out a gasp as I pull her closer. "You forgot to give me a kiss this morning."

She giggles. "A little presumptuous, isn't it?" However, her body tells a different story. Her chest rises and falls quickly, and she leans her head closer, her gaze flicking between my eyes and my mouth.

My lips curl up in a cocky smirk. "No. You'll kiss me by the end of the day." I tilt my head down to meet hers, our lips almost touching. I breathe her in and bask in her peppermint scent, the remnants of the candy cane she was undoubtedly sucking on moments earlier.

Leigh lifts her hand and traces along my jaw. "Maybe in your dreams. You've got a patient, doc." She slips out of my grip and saunters down the hallway, tossing me a glance over her shoulder before she turns the corner.

Fuck me.

It isn't until noon that I find myself alone with her. Her back is facing me as she stands in the break room, and I take a moment to enjoy her ass in those jeans. It jiggles as she taps her foot in sync with the song playing throughout the office. The microwave in front of her beeps, and she opens it, grabs her mug, and sets it on the counter. She reaches for the napkins and uses one to pick up two of the Christmas cookies Annie brought by this morning.

In three long strides, I capture my little mouse in front of me by placing my hands on both sides of her and caging her in against the counter. Her body stiffens against me. Then, leaning forward so my mouth is right beside her ear, I whisper, "Your lips on mine will be the best Christmas gift this year."

Some of the tension melts from her body as she cocks her head to the side. "Oh. I thought me tied in a bright red bow would be the best thing?"

A strand of hair falls in front of her face. I smooth it behind her ear, then gently graze her neck with my lips. She gasps at the contact and arches her back, leaning into my chest. My cock is hard and straining against the small of her back. It's all I can do not to grind into her.

"Playing with fire gets you burned, little mouse." I trail my tongue down her neck to her shoulder, then tug on her sleeve, revealing more skin and a small tattoo—a dark red heart with horns. A shiver rips through her as I nip her shoulder.

This will be fun.

The thought is fleeting, as Leigh twists away from me with a smirk. "You have no idea, boss." She winks, grabs her cookies and what smells like apple cider, then walks back toward the front of the office.

Still facing the counter, I palm my cock to release some tension. Unfortunately, it only makes me harder. And just when I think it can't get any worse, it does.

"Hello, Dr. Wilson." Shannon laughs as she slides next to me, reaches for a mug, and playfully bumps my shoulder. *Shit.*

"Hi, Shannon. I thought you weren't coming in today." I turn the opposite direction, hoping to hide my raging hard-on from my other receptionist.

She pours coffee into her cup, adds two sugar cubes, then stirs her coffee before answering. "Well, people tend to want to get paid, especially around the holidays. I'm just going to finish payroll, then I'm out of here. But since you're here, I wanted to discuss something with you."

"Sure. Is everything okay?"

Shannon waves her hand. "Oh, yes. It's just . . . I've noticed a little something between you and Leigh." I open my mouth to speak, but she holds up her hand. "I know it's not my place, but I see how you look at her. So, this is a friendly reminder that you're the boss. And Leigh is a good receptionist, not to mention a good friend. I don't want to see either of you get hurt."

"It's just a little holiday cheer, that's all. Nothing to worry about, Shannon." I plaster a fake smile on my face. There is definitely something to worry about. Leigh's stroking the fire inside me, and I'm dying to show her exactly what happens when you play with fire.

"You're my friend too, and I'd hate to see you abuse your power as her employer." We're close in age, but Shannon tries to mother everyone. As if I don't already have my pesky mother breathing down my throat with every little thing, and she's hundreds of miles away.

24

I nod. "Thank you. I appreciate you looking out for me. I'm taken, but there's no harm in looking."

"Oh, you are? I didn't realize." We've never talked about my marital status because I like to keep my life as private as possible. Crimson is a small town, but sometimes even the gossipiest person doesn't know everything. "I'm sorry I overstepped," she says.

"No worries. We're good." As I leave the room, her words resonate with me.

Shannon's right about one thing.

I am her boss. I make the rules, goddamn it. And Leigh will be mine, on her knees, begging for my cock before Christmas.

Chapter Five

Leigh

FRIDAY. TIME FOR THE last appointment of the week. I bounce my leg nervously and drum my fingers on the counter. There's no one else here—just me and the doctor.

I take a deep breath, then walk back toward his office. The door is open, but I knock anyway. He looks up, frustration shadowing his features. "Yes, Leigh?"

"You have one more patient today."

"I know. Why aren't they here yet?" he asks.

"I'm your last patient." I brace myself. For what, I'm not sure.

He raises a brow. "You are?"

I look down at the ground, finding the courage to speak. "I wasn't sure how to tell you since you're my boss. My usual gynecologist is out of the country, and it's time for my yearly exam."

He nods his understanding. "Okay. Go ahead to room one and undress. I'll be there in just a minute."

I walk into the patient room, where I've already laid out the necessary supplies. Quickly, I strip down to nothing and then cover myself as best I can with the paper gown and blanket. Counting the seconds, I get to forty-nine before Dr. Wilson knocks on the door. "You ready?"

"Yes. Come in."

"I'm sure you know the routine fairly well"—he snaps a glove on his wrist, causing me to jump—"but I'll still walk you through it before I do anything. We'll do the breast exam first. Lay down and raise your hands above your head." The gown falls partway open as I obey. "Have you been performing your monthly self-checks?"

"Yes, sir."

The cold air in the room circulates as Dr. Wilson shifts one side of the gown, exposing my puckered nipple. He has a tender but firm touch while he moves around one breast. The back of his hand brushes against my nipple, and shock runs through me. I take in a sharp breath and let it out slowly.

A woman's annual exam is one of the most embarrassing doctor's appointments. You think of anything you can to distract yourself from the exam. Everything about it screams *uncomfortable*. However, there's something about Dr. Wilson that puts me at ease. There's pain behind his green eyes, but his smile says he'll get through it. It stirs the wild in me, aching to bring it out of him too. His touch right now is gentle, yet I can't help but wonder what a rougher touch from him would feel like. How his hands would feel wrapped around my waist. What his lips would feel like against my hot skin.

He taps my leg, and it brings my focus back to the room. "Feet up, please." I was so lost in thought I didn't realize he completed the first part of the exam already and is now sitting on the chair by my feet, motioning to the stirrups.

"Sorry," I mumble. Stretching my legs out one at a time, I put my feet into the stirrups and scoot my butt down toward the end of the table. My lower half is completely exposed to him.

"Good girl."

It's so low I almost miss it. He clears his throat as he grabs the speculum and rubs it between his hands. "Hopefully this will warm it up a bit. You'll feel some pressure while I open you up, a quick pinch, and then we'll be done."

Something slippery touches me, then cold metal presses into me and clicks a couple of times. Before I can stop it, a moan falls from my lips. I quickly cover my mouth, hoping he didn't hear it.

"Naughty girl." He *tsks* at me. "That wasn't supposed to happen."

A blush creeps up my face, but I don't dare speak. As if this wasn't embarrassing enough, my body betrays me. I should not have thought about this striking man in front of me. I shake my head to ward off the thoughts, but it doesn't do much when I feel the pinch he mentioned. The same body that betrays me is the same body that jumps and writhes.

"Almost done," he says, squeezing my leg. A rough breath escapes my lips. His touch is electric, and it terrifies me.

"Oh, Leigh." He inches the speculum partway out, causing me to wince. "There, there . . . How does this feel?" Two fingers slide into me, rubbing the pinched area before he fully removes the speculum. My pussy clenches in response.

"Is this part of the exam?"

He presses that spot inside me harder. Once again, I can't stop the whimper from my mouth. Then, his fingers are sliding out, leaving me empty. My knees lean toward each other, but he nudges one leg with his elbow. Instinctively, I open my legs wider. I'm rewarded with another finger as he pushes back inside me.

"God, this cunt swallows me." His movements are lazy but deliberate, inducing a haze of lust through my body. "It's so greedy. Are you greedy, Leigh?"

"Sir?" My breath is ragged. I try to sit up to look at him, but my view is obstructed. Instead, his thumb hits my clit, and I fall back onto the table. He groans, slowly withdrawing his fingers.

"I've got you," he breathes, adding another. My hips buck on the table, and he puts a palm on my lower stomach to hold me down.

I clear my throat and try again. "Doctor?" My hips involuntarily buck when he removes his hand from my stomach and grabs the bottle of lube on the side tray.

He squeezes more, liberally coating his hand and wrist and twisting it to lube the skin around the hand that's still inside me. I prop myself up on my elbows to watch, and my breath catches in my throat when he tucks his thumb and slides his whole hand inside me.

"I don't think you're supposed to be doing this," I groan.

"What, this?" He flexes his fist a little, drawing a loud moan from me, then quickly pulls his fist out. Before the tips of his fingers leave my pussy, he shoves his fist back in.

"Doctor!" My voice sounds foreign to my ears—needy and wanton.

The doctor groans in appreciation. "Tell me you don't like it. Tell me to stop." He clenches his fist again, applying outward pressure against the walls of my pussy.

"You're my boss. We shouldn't do this."

"Call me Connor." He grips my leg and pumps his fist quickly in and out several times. "And I don't see anyone else here. Do you?"

The realization hits me like a cold splash of water to the face. My boss has his whole fist inside me after an embarrassing annual exam. This isn't professional. I should tell him to stop. But damn if this isn't something thrilling.

His eyes meet mine, and something wicked sparks inside them. Then, smirking, he says, "You're so wet, little mouse. Hear those sounds you make? Your sweet cunt is dripping for me." He slows his movements down, then leans forward and places open-mouthed kisses over my thigh.

"Oh, fuck," I cry out. "Connor!" As forbidden as this is, it's all I want. The desire for my boss consumes me.

Connor trails light kisses up my leg to my most sensitive part. Once he's there, he tongues my clit, pumping his fist faster.

I scream out my release, panting and writhing on the table. Before I come down from my orgasm, Connor is back to being all business.

He straightens his jacket, grabs the sample off the tray, and turns to face me. "You should get your results back within the week." He nods before exiting the exam room, then closes the door behind him.

Horrified, the embarrassment creeps back up my body and leaves me shivering. I can't decipher the look on his face before he left the room. It's as if what transpired between us is tearing him in half. By the time I clean myself up and get dressed, Dr. Wilson has left the building, taking a piece of my thumping heart with him.

Chapter Six

Connor

I KNOW IT WAS despicable to leave her exposed on the table, but what was I supposed to do? I breached my rules and my ethics by touching a patient inappropriately. A stunningly beautiful patient. A patient I feel an eminent pull toward. A patient who feels the same pull as I do.

One taste of her is not enough. It never will be enough.

I crossed that proverbial line, and there's no turning back. Watching her orgasm on the table will haunt my dreams. It's forbidden, unethical, and should make me feel disgusted as a doctor. But does it? It is forbidden and unethical, yes. And disgusted isn't exactly the word I would use to describe myself. Maybe sinful, compromised, and enchanted. Yes. Yes, I think so.

I can't deny the feelings Leigh stirs up inside of me. It's been a while since a woman has held my attention the way she does.

I'm an addict, and Leigh is a problem I just can't quit.

Quickly, I gather up my things from the office, lock the door, and slip out into the bitter, cold night before I convince her to come home with me. Unfortunately, the cold does nothing to stop my raging erection.

It takes my car a few minutes to warm up, and those minutes give me more time to imagine a fantasy life outside of work with Leigh. I can see us walking down Main Street, holding hands. She's excitedly talking about the Christmas lights and decorations with a cup of apple cider in her hand. Later, I see her bent over the kitchen counter, ass red from my hand, and her pussy soaking wet for me. Next, her belly is growing every day, carrying my child—starting the family I desperately want.

Fuck.

I want every single ounce of her. The good, the bad, and the dirty. I want it all.

By the time Monday morning rolls around, I'm grateful to leave my apartment. The quiet isn't something I think I'll ever get used to, and random noise doesn't cut it. My body aches to share the bed with someone, but my soul craves her presence. Tomorrow is Christmas, and Leigh hasn't been on her knees begging for my cock yet.

There's still time.

Annie greets me when I walk into the bakery. "Connor!"

Coffee. I just need coffee.

"Hey, Annie." I smile at her and walk toward the coffee.

"How's Leigh doing?"

"She's doing well. Definitely making my life easier. I should've hired her ages ago." Adding in the creamer, I stir the black liquid and see it turn lighter.

"Oh, is that so?" A hint of amusement drips from her words. "And how are you?"

I raise my brow. "Having fun?" I ask. She snickers as she plates some brownies. "Those for Lizzy?"

"Six months pregnant and all she wants are these damn brownies. Poor Tucker."

Good friends of mine, Tucker and Lizzy, got married six months ago, and she surprised him on their wedding day with the positive test. Annie's brownies are Lizzy's favorite dessert. Tucker proposed with brownies, and they had brownies at their wedding reception, so it's only fitting that she's craving brownies during her pregnancy.

"Can I get an apple cider to go?"

Annie rolls her eyes. "That the last piece of the puzzle?"

"I don't know what you are talking about. I think all that sugar is going to your head." I grin at her. While she pours the apple cider, I dig around in my pocket for a twenty-dollar bill. "Keep the change, Annie. Merry Christmas."

Rolling her eyes, she hands me the large cup, then nods. "Merry Christmas!"

When I walk into the office, the front desk is empty. I was in such a rush to leave on Friday that I hadn't checked the schedule for early appointments today. After hanging my coat up, I make my way through the building until I find her in the break room. She's bending down to retrieve something from the fridge's bottom shelf, giving me a delicious view of her ass. My eyes trail down her body and soak in her long legs. I stifle a groan and walk into the room. She hasn't noticed me yet.

Leigh closes the fridge and sidesteps to the counter. Closing the space between us, I reach up and weave my fingers through her hair, pulling tight at her nape and forcing her head to the side.

"Connor!" she gasps, dropping the bag of baby carrots on the counter. I set the apple cider down next to it.

My name falling from her lips is a godsend. A plea. A promise. A whisper straight to my cock.

"Good morning, Leigh," I grunt in her ear. "Why must you tease me with these skirts?" My other hand grips her outer thigh, grazing the hem of her skirt. "It's almost time for my gift."

"I didn't get you anything." Her laugh turns to a gasp when my tongue hits where her shoulder meets her neck.

"Your moans are all I need," I taunt. "You creaming all over my cock, screaming my name as you come. I bet you're wet right now, thinking about the dirty things we'll do later. Feel how hard you make me."

I guide her hand to my cock. She palms it, giving it a quick squeeze that elicits a groan from me.

Leigh runs her hand up and down my length, taking in short quick breaths as I tighten my grip on her hair. She's playing dangerously close to the fire, and there's not enough water in the office to hose us down. I buck my hips against her, needing that sweet release.

Ding ding ding.

We freeze when we hear the bell at the front desk. She releases my cock, twists out of my grip, and grabs the apple cider.

"Thanks for this," she says, holding up the drink, then disappears into the hallway.

Chapter Seven

Leigh

"LEIGH." HE KNOCKS ON the glass behind me to get my attention. "Come to my office when you're finished."

"You got it." I file the paper in the cabinet to my left and hand the other piece to Jack, the last patient of the day.

"Someone's in trouble," Jack teases.

I roll my eyes and laugh. "It's probably my Christmas bonus. No big deal."

He tosses me a smile. "Well, good luck!"

"Thanks," I say. "Let me walk you out." I grab the keys before stepping around the counter. When we reach the door, I hold it open for Jack and usher him out. "Merry Christmas, take care!"

Shutting the door firmly behind him, I latch both locks, then give it a push to double-check it's secured. On my way back to the desk, I tidy up the waiting room, straightening the chairs as I go. The lights dim right on schedule as I round the corner. It doesn't feel right to leave without tidying up, so I fix a few things on my desk, then grab my purse and coat and walk down the hall to Dr. Wilson's office.

Peeking my head in, I knock on the door.

"You wanted to see me?"

"Yes, come in." He stands up and leans against his desk, arms crossed.

I walk into the room and close the door behind me. He motions for me to come closer. Setting my stuff down on the chair beside the door, I slowly inch toward him until we're within arm's reach. My heart beats with anticipation as I wait for his direction. His green eyes meet mine, and my breath quickens as warmth spreads from my head to my toes. My scalp tingles as I remember how he grabbed my hair, taking complete control of me in the break room. In this moment, I'd do anything he asked. With my body flushed and my hands shaking, I wait for him to say something. *Anything.*

"Suck my cock, Leigh."

Without hesitation, I drop to my knees, unbuckle his belt, and slowly unzip his slacks. I let them fall to the ground before I pay attention to the massive length in front of me. His cock is rock hard and strains against his boxers. The pink tip pokes out, giving me a peek of the treat I'm in for. I've felt the bulge before, but seeing it up close and personal? It's impressive.

He groans as I drag the thin fabric away from him. His cock springs free, and I stick my tongue out to catch the bead of pre-cum glistening on his tip.

"Oh, fuck."

He lets out a long breath.

I open my mouth and let my lips close around him. His shaft twitches as I swirl my tongue around the tip. Relaxing my jaw, I take more of him into my mouth. He lets me set the pace and rock back and forth on my knees. I run my tongue down the length of his shaft, not quite reaching the base.

"Leigh," he pants as he thrusts his hips toward me. His cock hits the back of my throat, and I moan against the gag, then suck in my cheeks to slide off him. "Ah, fuck. Right there."

Connor's control snaps. He grabs the back of my head and pulls me closer to him. This time, when his cock hits the back of my throat, it slips down, but he quickly pulls out. He repeats the action twice before holding my head with both hands and fucking my mouth.

His thrusts are brutal and unrelenting, the tip dipping into my throat each time. Tears fill my eyes, but he doesn't stop. Saliva drips down my chin and onto my blouse. His moans fill the office as his cock twitches.

Suddenly, he pulls out, leaving me gasping for air. He loosens his tie and looks at me with lust-filled eyes. "Open up." Slowly, I open my sore mouth a little. Connor grabs my jaw and pries it open wider, then shoves the tie inside. "I said open. Now don't make a sound."

I shake my head in protest and use my tongue to try to push the tie out of my mouth. Instead, he pulls me up, spins me around, and bends me over his desk.

Smack!

His hand comes down on my ass *hard*. "Ahh!" I cry out, muffled by the tie.

"Not one sound."

I push off the desk and shove backward, pushing him away. He reaches out and grabs a fistful of hair, twisting my head to force me to look at him.

"I've wanted you from the day I laid eyes on you. Your dripping cunt knows who it belongs to, but just in case you have any doubts, I'm about to show you." His grip on my hair loosens just enough for me to relax, then he guides me back to his desk.

Connor growls in my ear as his hips pin me against the desk, still facing him. He tugs my blouse out of my skirt and grabs the bottom with both hands. In one swift motion, he rips my shirt. Buttons clatter across the desk and floor.

As he grinds against me, he whispers, "These gorgeous tits should never be concealed." He snakes a hand into my bra and pinches my nipple. My body twists away from him, but it only provokes him more, and now, with my back facing him, he's caged me in. I arch my ass against him and push off the desk with my hands, trying to gain leverage to push him away.

"Oh, no, you don't." He catches my arm again and twists it behind my back. "If you're not going to behave, I will make you." I hear a loud noise to my left and turn my head in time to see the indoor Christmas tree next to the window falling. The lights unravel more with each pull as Connor yanks them toward us. Within moments, he's using them to his advantage. I hiss as the hot bulbs press into my skin while he deftly wraps them around my wrists and arms.

Tears sting my eyes, and I whimper against the tie. With every tug of my wrists, the lights dig in a little more. A sinister chuckle close to my ear startles me, and it finally sinks in that the big bad wolf has caught his little mouse.

He pushes my skirt up and yanks down my underwear, then shoves my head flush against the desk and plunges into me. "Oh, fuck. You're so goddamn tight." The more he thrusts, the more my body betrays me. Again.

His hand reaches underneath me, touching the area where our bodies meet. "You love this, don't you? See how wet you are." Glistening fingers graze my cheek, and I try to move my head away, but he has a hold on the nape of my neck, pinning me in place. "Why don't you be a good girl for me, Leigh? Take it. That's it . . ."

I know how much my body enjoys this. I know I'm soaking wet and gripping his cock tightly. Just like I know Connor will make me come long and hard, and then he'll continue to use my body until he's finished.

This time, his fingers find my clit, and he pinches it. I squirm under him, but he only adds more pressure and slams my head on the desk again. I cry out against the tie and wriggle my wrists. The lights dig in harder, and the pain in my arms combined with the pain in my head fills my eyes with tears.

The weight of his body comes down on mine as his thrusts slow. "You're doing so good, baby. Taking every inch of my cock. Such a good girl." Connor whispers in my ear as he grabs my throat. He applies pressure and continues to fuck me slowly.

He warned me. *Playing with fire gets you burned.*

My body is in agony. Restricted airflow, fabric in my mouth, and my arms tied behind my back, yet my body still gives in. Betrays me.

Proves to Connor just how much I want this.

How much I like being fucked and discarded like a whore.

How slick my pussy is for him.

How much I want him and only him.

It's over. And he fucking knows it.

His grip on my throat tightens, and he bites down on my shoulder as he bucks his hips harder into me.

Pain. Pleasure. Bliss. I cry out as his assault on my senses comes to a head all at once. Dr. Connor fucking Wilson will be my undoing.

Chapter Eight

Connor

AS MANY TIMES AS I've imagined this moment—Leigh writhing under me, bound and gagged, milking my cock—my imagination never did it justice.

The look of pure ecstasy shines through her features, and excitement seeps through her pores.

She's tried to deny this force between us. She's tried to escape me. But there's no escaping this.

Leigh is mine. All fucking mine.

Her pussy squeezes my cock, kick-starting my orgasm. I slow my thrusts, drawing out the immense pleasure floating through my body. She's shaking underneath me, but I'm not done with her yet.

Releasing my grip on her throat, I reach up to remove the tie from her mouth. She takes a huge breath and lets it out in a rush. There's no time for more because my hand flies back to her throat, and I pull her torso up to me. I tilt her head up and greedily capture her lips.

A second orgasm rips through her body, and I fuck her with complete abandon. She parts her lips, and my tongue darts in to taste her. Our moans mingle, and I can't tell where mine start and hers end.

Tasting her isn't enough. Fucking her isn't enough. Nothing will ever be enough.

I give her every last drop of my cum, claiming her body once and for all. Then, finally satisfied, we pull away, and she lies back on the desk, panting. She flinches when I untangle the lights from her wrists, then moans a sigh of relief and rubs at her arms.

"Thank you," she pants.

"You say that like we're done." A devilish smile creeps across my face. "I'm never done with you, Leigh." I spank her ass for good measure, then help her stand.

She spins around on those heels that drive me wild and wraps her arms around my neck with a sly smile. "That's what you think, boss."

I growl and grab her waist, hoisting her up onto the desk. "Test me, little mouse. I dare you." She squirms under my gaze and falls silent. Closing the small gap between us, I nip her bottom lip. Her fingers tangle in my hair, and she lets out a long whimper.

My cock hardens at her sweet sounds. Our tongues are in a game of war to see who comes out on top. I pinch her nipple and roll it between my thumb and forefinger as I drag my other hand up her thigh. My heart swells with joy when she breaks the kiss to release a loud moan.

"Do you not like my gift? You're dripping." I swipe some of her juices off the desk and show her. "Show me how much you like it."

Our eyes lock when she grabs my hand with both of hers and slowly brings it to her mouth. Her tongue darts out, tasting the sweet liquid. Then she closes her mouth around my finger and moans as she swirls her tongue. Her eyes don't leave mine for a second as she cleans my finger.

She releases my finger with a *pop*, then smirks at me. "Better?"

I break eye contact and look down at the desk between her legs. *What a lovely mess.* Using two fingers this time, I gather up the last of the mess and shove my fingers inside her swollen pussy. She gasps at the contact and clenches around me.

Her hips buck against my hand as she cries out. "Yes, oh fuck."

Damn. I'll never get enough of the way she looks. I am addicted to Leigh and her sweet sounds.

"More," she pants. I add a third finger and pump in and out several times, feeling my dick harden again. Just when she's right on edge, I slow my motions, then stop entirely. "Don't stop, Connor," she whimpers.

In one swift movement, I plunge my cock into her wet pussy, and the weeks of tension fade away. "Oh, little mouse. Never." She meets me thrust for thrust as we both climb toward another climax. "You're mine. Say it."

"Yours," she breathes into my ear.

The woman who was made just for me falls apart as the orgasm shatters through her, dragging me with her into perpetual bliss.

There's a soft knock at the door before it flies open. I glance up in time to see the look of pure shock and horror on Shannon's face, her jaw just about hitting the floor.

I reach around me to the back of my chair and grab my coat, wrapping it around Leigh before pulling away. Shannon turns around while I quickly re-dress. She still hasn't said a word, but it's clear she's not leaving unless I go with her. I place a small kiss on Leigh's forehead.

Clearing my throat, I step out from behind the desk. "Ah, my wife is such a good girl, isn't she?"

Chapter Nine

Connor

THE OFFICE DOOR CLOSES behind me, and the second it does, Shannon shrieks, "Your wife?!"

I smirk at her before answering. "Well, I did tell you I was taken. Happily married, in fact."

"Why didn't you tell me?" Her signature look of disapproval dons her eyes.

"Because marriage can be ugly. I know ours is. It's not a promise to love someone until you stop; it's a promise to make a conscious decision every day to love someone, even when it's hard. We're both a mess at times, but she's my rock." I look back at the closed door, then back to Shannon. "We've had our fair share of problems, and some days it feels like we're starting over. It's hard to break that."

Her gaze softens, and she shakes her head. "You should have told me. I must've looked like a fool."

"Your heart was in the right place." I chuckle. "I thought you weren't coming in today?"

"I wasn't, but I forgot to leave the gifts when I was here the other day. One for each of you, in the break room. Wait . . . don't tell me you did it there too?"

Not yet. "No, your precious lunch table is fine."

"Merry Christmas, Leigh!" she yells through the door, then turns to me. "Merry Christmas, Dr. Wilson. I'll see you on the second."

"The second?" That's over a week from now.

She laughs and stalks down the hall toward the front door.

"Shannon, why the second?"

"After what I just witnessed, I deserve an extended holiday." She waves and then walks around the corner.

I'm grinning like a fool when I open my office door but stop dead in my tracks. *Holy fuck.* Leigh is facing me, spread-eagle on my desk, wearing nothing but her heels and my stethoscope around her neck. My eyes darken as I zero in on her hand. Slowly, she dips a finger into her pussy and tips her head back.

"You've been a naughty little mouse, haven't you?" I softly close the door behind me.

She shudders at my words as she adds another finger. "Yes. What are you going to do about it?" Leigh taunts me, unleashing the wolf inside me like she can't wait for me to catch her.

I take my time to undress as Leigh's soft moans fill the room, and I wait for my moment to pounce. She alternates between her pussy and clit, smearing the wetness between her folds. Groaning in appreciation, I close the distance between us and fall to my knees.

Her scent hits my nose, filling me with hunger and lust. Placing my hands on her ass, I scoot her closer to the edge before biting her inner thigh. She grips the edge of the desk to steady herself.

"Fuck," she breathes. "Connor, please."

I spread her lips and dart my tongue out, connecting with her clit. Her fingers tug at my hair, encouraging me. My fingers slide into her pussy, and she bucks her hips.

"Yes."

Leigh's moans get louder as my assault on her pussy continues. I nip at her clit. She pulls my head closer and grinds on my face, using me for her pleasure. She screams my name when she reaches her climax and sobs rack her body. I trail kisses up her stomach, her chest, her neck, not stopping until I get to her lips. They part, an invitation to consume her.

Our tongues mingle slowly, exploring everything we can. A growl rips through my chest as I plunge into the sweetest part of her. Everything slows down and fades away until the only things left are us. This time is different. This time, I fuck her deliberately, slowly, clinging to her as though it's been days since I've had her pussy. Days. Weeks. Months. Because it has been.

It's been eighteen months since I fucked up. Eighteen agonizing months since we've slept in the same bed. Five hundred and forty-seven nights of silence. Today is the first day in eighteen months I have felt whole.

I am my best person with her by my side. I'm so desperately and hopelessly in love with Leigh, and I will spend the rest of my life proving it to her, no matter how long it takes.

Her sweet voice fills my ear with the one thing I've been aching to hear. "Connor, take me home."

Epilogue

Leigh

THREE MONTHS LATER . . .

"Both of you have made tremendous progress. I'm glad you're working through this." Our marriage counselor sits across from us in a chair. "There's been open and honest communication on both sides. I'm proud of you."

Connor grabs my hand and gives it a reassuring squeeze. "It's been difficult, but I've been sticking to the program and really getting some help. I'm being accountable and taking responsibility for the damage I caused."

I clear my throat before speaking. "As you know, we started sleeping together again at Christmas. I was hesitant at first because of what you said. But, at some point, we had to reintegrate sex back into our relationship. Every day since then, I've felt nothing but adoration from the man I married. The feelings of uncertainty are gone. There hasn't been any more second-guesses, and we're getting back into the rhythm of married life." I glance at Connor and smile. "It's been hard, but our marriage is worth it."

Sex blurs the lines when you're in recovery. It can be hard on the addict, but it can be equally hard on their partner. Aside from living apart for a while, taking sex off the table was the next thing we needed to do, especially during the early stages of Connor's sobriety. It's an intricate part of our lives—we'd have sex almost daily. Getting him to admit he has a drinking problem wasn't a small feat.

His father is an alcoholic, as was his grandfather, and his grandfather's father. Alcoholism runs in his family. I knew that when I married him, and I know it's something he'll battle for the rest of his life. I thank my lucky stars every day I'm able to help him through his recovery and be a cheerleader for him every step of the way. Marriages can survive alcoholism and sobriety, and ours will be one of them.

"That's good to hear." The counselor nods her head. "At this point, I believe therapy has run its course. You are more than welcome to continue coming back, but I don't think you need it. Practice what you've learned, and remember to understand that you will have different perspectives at times, and that's okay. Disagreements are inevitable in every relationship, but how you handle them will make all the difference." She stands to signal the end of our session.

"Thank you," Connor says as he stands up to shake her hand. "I don't think we would have gotten through this without you."

During our separation, I discovered a lot about myself and our relationship. I've grown emotionally, cried buckets of tears, and learned to depend on myself. I stayed in our home while Connor rented an apartment after his sabbatical from work for rehab. The silence was sometimes deafening, but I had to learn to trust the process. Letting Connor go paved the way for us to start over.

At the car, he opens the door for me, just like he used to when we first started dating. Some habits never die. I climb into the car with a smile and place a gentle hand on my belly.

This little one is the Christmas miracle we didn't know we needed.

The End

Ricky: Listen, Fred, I've got an awful problem on my hands.

Fred: You should have thought about that before you married her.

I Love Lucy - Season 1 Episode 27

Naughty Doctor Playlist

Long Hair and Some Tattoos by Bryce Savage

No Longer Broken by Alphamega

Untouchable by Atreyu

Play With Fire by Sam Tinnesz

Sleigh Ride by Tori Kelly

Appetite by Nathan James

Beautiful Way by You Me At Six

Blow by Eva Under Fire (ft Ice Nine Kills)

Just Pretend by Bad Omens

All I Want For Christmas Is You by Mariah Carey

I Do by Paul Brandt

Leigh and Connor's Recipes

Homemade Apple Cider

10-12 medium apples (assorted types), quartered

2 oranges, quartered (peeled*)

4 cinnamon sticks**

1 tablespoon whole cloves**

Water

½ brown sugar (to taste)

Extras:

Fine-mesh strainer

Wooden spoon

Huge pot (stockpot or crock pot***)

1. Wash, core, and cut the apples. Place the quartered apples into the pot.

2. Cut and peel oranges. Place them in the pot with the apples.

3. Add the spices to the pot, then cover everything with water. Leave about an inch or two of space at the top.

4. Cover the pot and let simmer until the apples are soft. Stockpot: 2 hours. Crockpot: high for 3-4 or low for 6-8.

5. Mash the apples and oranges. Using the wooden spoon, take a minute to mash all the apples and oranges against the side of the pot to release more of their flavor. Then cover it again, and let it simmer for a little while longer.

6. Using a fine-mesh strainer, strain out the solids (apples, oranges, spices) back into the pot by pressing them against the strainer. Discard the solids when finished.

7. Stir in the desired sweetener, to taste. Serve warm.

*Peeling the oranges will reduce the tartness in the cider. Leave unpeeled if desired.

**Dried powdered spices work too, whichever is easiest or on hand. Nutmeg can be a great addition if desired.

***If using a smaller pot, halve the recipe for best results.

Cut Out Cookies

1 cup butter, softened

1 cup sugar

1 tsp vanilla extract

½ tsp almond extract

1 egg

2 tsp baking powder

3 cups flour

Extras:

Wax paper

Rolling pin

Cookie cutters

Sprinkles and/or frosting for decorating

1. In a medium bowl, mix the flour and baking powder. Set aside.

2. Cream the butter and sugar until light and fluffy in a mixing bowl. Add in the extracts and the egg. Mix until incorporated.

3. Slowly add the dry ingredients and mix well. If the dough becomes too thick for the mixer, take it out of the bowl and mix it by hand.

4. Preheat the oven to 350° F.

5. Divide the dough in half and put one-half between two pieces of wax paper. Roll the dough between the paper until desired thickness*.

6. Cut the dough using cookie cutters or a knife. Top with sprinkles if desired.

7. Bake for 6-8 minutes**. They should lightly bounce back when you push the center.

8. Let the cookies cool on a baking rack if frosting is desired. They should be cool to the touch before frosting.

*Desired thickness is best at ¼ inch but can be left up to preference.

**You don't want the cookies to be brown. They should stay golden as they will continue to cook as they cool.

Countdown Madness

by Zoey Zane
Sneak Peek

Thanks for reading Naughty Doctor! Did you enjoy Connor and Leigh's story? Please consider leaving a review on Amazon and Goodreads! Continue reading for a sneak peek of Countdown Madness, available now!

Chapter One

STORMS ARE ONE OF the things I love most about Crimson, but what I love even more is what comes after the rain. Petrichor: the best smell in the whole world.

As I watch the mist that hugs the mountains, serenity washes over me. Many people fear storms, running away scared of what they bring. I run into a storm, begging it to calm my inner chaos until all is silent.

Standing up, I drape the blanket on the back of the bench and walk to the mailbox, realizing I never checked yesterday's mail. The mailbox is slightly ajar, leaving the corner of a large manila envelope peeking out. I open the mailbox, curious about what it is. A couple of bills and a magazine, but nothing else catches my attention.

As I slide the flap open, I peer into the envelope. There's a smaller envelope with something hard at the bottom. I turn it upside down and a key falls out. Turning over the key, I notice there's nothing on it. It's just a simple key. Reaching back into the manila envelope, I tug out a smaller envelope with the number ten written on it and rip it open. The note reads:

Here comes your next adventure. There will be a series of clues, beginning with this one. It will serve as your countdown to the day your big adventure begins. It is yours for the taking.

The next clue is where you went when things got tough at home. No friends, no neighbors, no family. Just you and your favorite thing.

"What the?" I mutter, confused. Turning the card over, there's no signature. I glance back at the envelope. There's no return address either. Just a postmark from the Crimson Post Office.

What the fuck? It's local, but who knows about my home life? I keep details of my childhood pretty tight-lipped when I can. However, there are some things I'd rather not talk about.

Puzzled, I walk back up to the porch and set the rest of the mail down on the table. I sit down on the couch and set the note on my lap. As I pick up my coffee and take a drink, I reread the postcard again and again, then switch between examining the big envelope and the small one. There's absolutely nothing on either one. No hints, no clues, nothing to tell me who sent this. After I finish the rest of my coffee, I make a decision. What's the worst that could happen?

The roads are wet, but there's not a lot of traffic this morning. My drive into town is short, and I don't have time to talk myself out of this. Before I know it, I'm parking my car in the lot by Crimson Credit Union. I take a deep breath and get out of the car. It's such a beautiful morning, and normally I'd enjoy it. But now, I rush into the bookstore, where Julie talks to Mr. Leon, the owner.

"Hello, Elizabeth!" Mr. Leon calls out.

I wave, not bothering to say hi back. I'm focused on one thing.

"Where is it?" I mutter, searching the shelves. It appears as though Mr. Leon has done some rearranging recently, making it more difficult to find the one I'm looking for.

When I was a young girl, I would spend countless hours in the children's section of the bookstore, reading every book I could get my hands on. My parents fought endlessly, right up until the moment my mother died. My mom worked at the credit union as a teller, back when it first opened. It was her first job, just like it was my first job. Because of my mom, I fell in love with numbers.

"There it is!"

I find my favorite book, ignoring that there is more than one copy. As I open it, a purple envelope falls out, and I chuckle. *Damn, I'm good.* Scooping up the paper, I see a nine written on it. I open the envelope, pull out the notecard, and see another clue.

Yay! You found me. You have officially begun the hunt for your true happiness. Here is the second clue.

I am made of red bricks where people see my friends fly. While many have suffered, the pretty colors fly high.

There's only one place where colors fly high in this town. Crimson Town Hall. Shaking my head, I walk back up to the front to chat with Julie.

I wave the notecard, and Julie raises her eyebrows.

"Hey, Lizzy. What's that?"

"You don't know?" She shakes her head. "I don't either." Laughing, I pull the first envelope out of my back pocket and hand it to her.

"A note?" she asks.

"Open it."

Julie hesitantly opens the envelope and pulls out the postcard. "Ten?"

"Turn it over."

She turns the card over in her hand and reads. Julie looks up at me, then looks back at the card. She reads it again. "And you're doing this?" she asks.

Silently, I hand her the second card.

Finally, Julie speaks. "I'm not sure what to make of it."

"That's what I'm thinking! Then I come here and find that. I mean, we live in a small town, so not many people would do something like this." My hands fly around—they move a lot when I talk. "Am I crazy?"

"I say, go for it! Who knows? Maybe Ethan has something up his sleeve?"

"I doubt it. He's not the type of guy to plan surprises." I huff and roll my eyes.

"Yeah, I can see that. He does have a stick up his ass, you know." She snorts, and a chuckle escapes me.

"Yeah, yeah."

"He's better once you get to know him," we say at the same time. Julie and Moxie always tease me about being with Ethan after so long. I have the itch for adventure—to experience the most I can out of life. Unfortunately, Ethan does not.

We've been engaged for six months, and while I hoped the engagement would ruffle his feathers or something, he acts disinterested, in a way. He's dragging his feet and wants to put things off for another year. It's difficult to plan a wedding when there's no date set.

Julie interrupts my wedding thoughts. "If it's not Ethan, do you know who it could be?"

"No idea." I shake my head. "I wouldn't even know where to begin!"

"Just be careful. Don't get tangled up in something you can't get out of. Crazies lurk everywhere."

"Yes, Mom." I laugh and walk toward the front of the store. "Well, I'm off to the town hall for the next clue. Call me later?"

"I'll be dying to know what happens!" she calls after me.

A sense of calm washes over me as I leave the bookstore. Julie is the level-headed one in my small group of friends, and while she's my age, she acts much older. Like me, we both have sick parents who require a great deal of care.

I'm hoping the clues are all in town. As long as they don't ask me to jump off a cliff or anything, I think I'll be fine. It is odd, though. Just in case, I pull out my phone and send Ethan a text.

Hi! Did you send me something in the mail? A manila envelope with a key? This is crazy! Call me before you head to work!

A few minutes later, on the outskirts of town, I arrive at the town hall. It was built in the early 1900s using only pure-red bricks. The American flag flies high in the air, secured to the pole standing to the right of the building. Behind the flag is

Memorial Cemetery. Usually, I stop to admire the cemetery, see the flowers, and say a prayer for the ones we've lost—like my mom's brother, who died in Vietnam. But today, I can't stop.

Making my way into the building, I scan the area, searching for anything that would indicate where the clue is. Nothing stands out. I blindly turn a corner and smack right into Ernie, the security guard.

"Oof!"

"Oh my god, Ernie! I'm so sorry!" Ernie laughs, and I turn to make sure he's all right.

He waves me off and says, "I was wondering when you'd come in. I have something for you."

I give him a curious look and follow him down the hall to his desk. He sits down, opens the bottom drawer, and pulls out a blue envelope. "I believe this belongs to you."

"Where did this come from?" I ask. With a hand that's shaking—with excitement or uncertainty, I'm not sure—I take it from him. I turn over the envelope and see the number eight. "How long have you had this?"

"Don't be a buzzkill, Lizzy. You'll ruin the fun." He winks.

Groaning, I pull out the postcard. "Well, at least that confirms something bad isn't at the end of this."

Ernie laughs and slams a hand down on the counter. "Don't you worry, young lady. You'll be fine."

Glancing at the postcard, I realize it's the same handwriting as the purple and white ones. The handwriting doesn't seem familiar, but it's a beautiful cursive font, like an elegant calligraphy.

I am full of the wind. I am a butterfly. I'm where your first kiss happened. Where am I?

My first kiss . . . a butterfly . . . oh my god, the school!

"Thank you, Ernie!" I lean over the counter and kiss his cheek.

"Good luck!" He smiles with a twinkle in his eye.

Okay, this has got to be Ethan. We were talking about first kisses and first loves just the other day. What's he doing? We're already engaged. Did he get promoted? No. It's not my birthday, and it's not my mom's either. It's not our anniversary. What is this?! Oh man, I'm kind of excited!

Crimson has been home for my entire twenty-six years on this earth. There's only one place I can think of with butterflies—the football field of the primary school. We only have two schools in Crimson—Butterflies: the years K-8 primary school, and Cardinals: the years 9-12 secondary school.

When I pull up to the Butterflies school, memories of my first kiss come rushing back. It was right before school let out for the summer, just after my fifteenth birthday. Tucker, my best friend, was my first kiss. I had been complaining that I didn't want to start high school without having been kissed. My father was sending me to a summer camp to get me out of his hair, and I remember rambling on and on about being the last to experience anything and how much I didn't want to die a virgin, even though a simple kiss wasn't the same thing as my virginity. Extreme for a fifteen-year-old, yes, but everything feels life-altering at that age. Maybe to shut me up, or maybe to help, I'm not sure, but Tucker grabs my waist and pulls me in for a panty-melting kiss. I had read about it in books and heard friends talk about it, but never experienced it until Tucker.

Most first kisses are messy, sloppy, and useless. But not mine. Mine was an earth-shattering, stuck-in-your-brain kiss—one you'll relive every time you kiss someone else. Until that day, I never saw Tucker as anything other than my best friend. For better or worse, he changed my life. I've had other kisses since then, and I'm not going to die a virgin, but there was never a match for Tucker's kiss. Nothing measures up to that high bar that I'm sure I'll never reach again.

Lost in thought, I wander around the field until I reach the bleachers. Taped to the handrail of the stairs, I see a pink envelope. Once again, a beautiful script greets me.

Memories can be manipulated over time, but this one you'll never lose. From age three to ninety-nine, I'll always stay. Come find me.

Riddles have never been my thing, but this one didn't even take me a second. It's referring to my childhood home, where I first learned of my parents' divorce.

Looking back, I can easily see how they came to the conclusion that they needed to separate. Sure, it was devastating, especially for an eight-year-old. But it was time for them. Jogging back to my car, my heart hurts a little, knowing where I'm heading next.

It's easy to say now they should have gotten divorced sooner. It's easy to think about two Christmases, two birthdays, two of everything. What's not easy is knowing it never happened due to unforeseen circumstances. It's not easy watching my father drown his sorrows in a bottle because he picked a fight with my mom the day she died in a car accident caused by a ruptured brain aneurysm on her birthday. It's not easy being a little girl and trying to pick up the pieces. And it definitely wasn't easy being on my own on that day, and on the anniversary of that day, even years later.

I've only been back to my childhood home twice since he sold it all those years ago. We stayed in it for a couple of years after Mom died, but it was too hard to keep living there. Father started drinking, lost his job, and got behind on the bills. He sold our house to pay them, and we moved into a tiny apartment across town. That's where I met Tucker. He was my next-door neighbor.

We finished growing up together and have been inseparable ever since. Amy—Tucker's mom—helped take care of me when my father couldn't. I spent many nights on their couch to avoid my father's drunken rage. She also taught me all the girly things you learn from your mom. She could never replace my mom, but it helped to have someone close to talk to. Amy and Tucker became my second family.

That's why my first kiss took me by such surprise. It never occurred to me that I could be in love with Tucker.

I didn't swoon over him the way other girls did. He was my best friend, who knew all my secrets, and I knew all of his. Until that fiery moment, I had only *thought* I knew what lust was. Tucker lit me up in all the right places, places I didn't know existed. Cliché, I know, but that kiss changed my life forever.

Pulling up to the house, I notice the owners haven't been taking care of the place. *Does anyone even live here anymore?* Plants are overgrown and are attempting to take over the porch. Tears fill my eyes, and I blink furiously to stop them from falling. I sit in my car for a few minutes before getting out and walking to the mailbox. There's a huge stack of mail, like the owners didn't leave a forwarding address. Sitting right on top is a green envelope with the number six written on it. I quickly tear it open:

Beyond the score of your childhood, beyond the scope of your reality, you've always dreamed of leaving. Find me where you've always wanted to go.

This one is tough. Sighing, I walk back to my car, noticing it's much later than I realized. It's time to call it a night.

Driving in the direction of home, my stomach growls. Amy—my surrogate mom—still loves to keep me fed. I've got a huge bowl of homemade mac and cheese waiting for me when I get home.

The drive home doesn't take as long as it normally does. After pulling into the driveway, I climb out of the car and walk up to the front porch, where I left the rest of the mail, my morning coffee, and the blanket. I pick everything up, unlock the door, and walk inside.

While I wait for my dinner to heat up, I start my nightly 15-minute clutter purge. It's silly to Tucker—he thinks I should live in a "lived-in" house. I argue that my place *is* lived in, but I like it to be picked up. All the things lying on the floor and the counters drive me crazy.

Tucker gives me the most shit for it when he comes over. He'll deliberately leave the pillow on the windowsill instead of putting it back on the couch because he knows it drives me up the wall. I chuckle at the thought of throwing the pillow at him.

The timer dings to let me know dinner is ready. I grab the bowl out of the oven, pick up my soda, and settle on the couch. I glance at my phone. I'm dying to call Ethan to tell him what's going on, but he hates it when I interrupt his business dinners. There are no texts or missed calls from him. Before I can second-guess myself, I decide to send him some quick texts.

You didn't text me before work as you always do. Hope everything is ok.

I have exciting news! I'm moving further along in the hunt – this is so fun! What have you gotten me into?

Can't wait to see you, call me soon so we can talk! Love you, babe.

I place the phone back on the coffee table and put my feet up as I press play. *Definitely, Maybe* with Ryan Reynolds lights up the living room in the otherwise dark house.

It's been an emotional day. A feel-good movie, feel-good food, and being cuddled up in the softest blanket known to man is exactly what I need right now.

Chapter Two

Lizzy

"Oww!" I CRY OUT, my body desperately in need of a good stretch as I shift my position on the couch. I can't believe I didn't get up last night. As I twist my limbs into comfortable positions and my muscles relax, a sense of relief flows through me. My breathing has slowed, and the raindrops outside seem louder, like the sound is coming from inside my house.

My phone vibrates against the coffee table. Tucker's face greets me, and I slide my finger across the screen to answer.

"It's so early," I groan.

"Well, good morning, Sunshine!" He chuckles. "What are your plans today?"

"Actually . . ." I pause. I really wanted to tell Ethan first, but he never texted me back last night. "I'm on a scavenger hunt."

"Oh, really?"

"It's really weird, though—"

"What? What do you mean?"

"Okay, so, I checked the mail yesterday—I didn't check it the day before, so I'm not sure how long it's been sitting in the mailbox—but there was a manila envelope with another envelope inside it labeled with the number ten and a key. I have no idea what the key is or where it leads to, but I'm hoping these clues will tell me."

"A key? Clues?" He doesn't like it when I talk a mile a minute.

"Yes, Tucker, keep up!" Laughing, I continue. "The first clue led me to the bookstore, where I found the second clue. That one lead me to the town hall. Then, the next clue took me to Butterflies. And I'm not done."

"You're not?" His laugh is music to my ears. "How surprising."

Sitting up on the couch, I gaze out the window to admire the view. The mountains are covered in darkness, rain cascades down in waves, and nothing is better than the scene before me. The appearance of beauty comes from the soul. Not many people enjoy the rain or storms in general, but me? I'm here for it all.

I take a breath and continue. "Nope. That last clue actually took me to the bleachers where you kissed me." My heart flutters when I hear his sharp intake of breath, but it shouldn't. I'm with Ethan, and Tucker and I aren't a thing. We can't be. We'll never be. I can't imagine my life without Tucker: my best friend, my favorite person.

"Next, the clue from the bleachers led me home. Well, to my parents' home. From before. And oh, shit. I forgot to tell you! Whoever owns it now is not taking care of it. There were overgrown plants, and honestly, it just looks trashy. I'm a little hurt by it, which I know is ridiculous, but I can't help it. That's where I remember my mom the most, you know?"

"Oh, Lizzy. That's not ridiculous," he says sadly.

"It is, but okay." I roll my eyes. "Their mailbox was almost overflowing with mail. Like, who doesn't leave a forwarding address? Is that something you can check on for me? Who sold it and just left it? Please, Tucker?" I don't bother to let him reply before moving on. "So, on top of that huge stack was another frigging envelope. I open it up and it says something about a place I've always dreamt of going to. That's where the next clue will be. The only thing I can think of is Italy, but there's no way I can fly across the world at a moment's notice just for a damn clue."

He's laughing again. "Lizzy."

"What?" A chuckle leaves my mouth too.

"Slow down, Sunshine. No, you're not traveling across the world for a clue. That could be dangerous. Was there a name on the clues? Do you even know where they're coming from?"

"Wait. You don't know?" I ask seriously. "It's Ethan! Come on, it's gotta be!"

Silence.

"Tucker, you there?"

He clears his throat. "I'm here."

"Good. Anyway, this last one has me stumped. I came home after that last clue and have been thinking about it all night, snuggled up with a good blanket, food, and a movie just to clear my head. I mean, come on. We know if I fixate on it, I'll never figure it out—I have to take a breather. So now you're all caught up. What do you think?"

"I think you need to be careful," he says.

"What do you think is going to happen? It's Ethan!"

He sighs. "You know how I feel about him."

"Come with me! It'll be fun."

"Just be careful is all I'm saying."

"Yes, sir."

Tucker lets out a small groan. "Lizzy."

"What?"

"Uh—nothing. It's okay."

"Just be happy for me. Ethan will be at the end of this with a thousand yellow daisies and candles, and it'll be amazing."

Silence.

"I need to go," Tucker says. "We'll talk later, okay?"

"Wait, Tuck—" The line goes dead.

What's his problem? I shake off the negative thoughts. *Today will be a good day, I just know it.*

Italy. Italy. Italy. It keeps repeating over and over again in my mind as I go through the day. I'm preoccupied at work with spreadsheet after spreadsheet after spreadsheet. Spreadsheets are one of my happy places, but I still can't concentrate. People can murky the waters, but numbers are the calm within the storm. When the ledger or balance sheet aligns and each side matches, its pluses and minuses the same, the chaos of the world slips away.

A million thoughts run through my head as each hour passes, and I'm becoming more frustrated. I push away the keyboard and turn off the monitors. After quickly grabbing my things, I head into Melanie's office.

I peek my head in. "Hey, I'm heading out early today. Gotta run some errands," I say. I've only been here for a couple of hours.

Without glancing up from her notebook, she says, "Great, have a good night!"

The rain has let up a little as I make my way to my car. It's a small drizzle now compared to the downpour it was this morning. I start the car and drive toward home, but partway there, I slam on the brakes.

Wait! If I can't go to Italy, I'll make Italy come to me. It's the only option! I make a U-turn. There's only one Italian restaurant in town. They make the best lasagna, almost as if they import it straight from Italy.

It's not too busy when I pull into the parking lot. I head inside and greet the owner, Milo, an older gentleman.

He smiles and asks, "The usual, to go?"

My stomach grumbles in response. "Yes, please. I guess I forgot to eat breakfast today."

"Be out in ten!" he says.

Glancing around me, I take in my surroundings. The only thing that looks different is the bulletin board. There's a huge map of Italy with an orange envelope pinned to Venice, the number five in that familiar, curly script on the front. I walk over to it and pull the pin out. *It has to be for me.* Putting the pin back in its place, I slide the envelope into my back pocket and take a seat.

Milo comes around the corner soon after, bringing a delicious smell with him. "I put some extra rolls in there for you."

"Oh, thank you! You're so good to me, Milo!" I slide him a twenty-dollar bill. "Keep the change."

As soon as I make it safely back into my car, I set the lasagna on the passenger seat and open the envelope.

Skipped rocks fall to their death, which is where I am. Can you find me?

A scoff escapes my lips. "Falling to their death? What?" *Oh my god. Ethan is crazy.* This riddle is too easy—there's only one place where you can skip rocks in Crimson. The lake. It's also a great place to eat lunch. There's a covered picnic area to shield me from the rain.

It was one of my favorite places to go in high school. I've spent many summers and fall nights there, enjoying the weather, cuddling up to the bonfire when it got colder, and roasting marshmallows with friends.

The lake is where I learned to swim, to steer a boat, and to water ski. So much laughter and good memories come flooding back during the drive there.

The parking lot is deserted when I arrive. Not even the boaters are out today, not that I blame them. I think I'm one of the only ones that actually crave the rain and everything that comes with it. When I come upon the picnic tables, I spot a black envelope taped to a pole. *Number four.* Shaking my head, I can't help myself. I tear it open to find the next clue.

Almost there. While I am here, they are all there. The place where couples go.

Ha, that's easy too! Make-out Point! My younger self did spend many nights there. Every town had one, even small ones like Crimson.

Excitement courses through my body. My stomach grumbles again, reminding me I haven't eaten yet. I sit down on the bench and eat. *It's so good.* Milo definitely knows how to make the best, most authentic lasagna. He is from Italy, after all.

The rain echoes off the tin roof. I could listen to that sound all day. Within a few minutes, I eat everything Milo made. The extra rolls were just what I needed to finish off the meal. I toss my garbage into the trash can and jog back to the car to keep myself from getting too wet.

I'm almost home with the clue from Make-out Point when it occurs to me. I still haven't heard from Ethan today. No texts, no calls, nothing. Which is odd, considering he usually texts me throughout the day. I've been caught up in the hunt, and I didn't realize I hadn't heard from him.

Instead of turning down the road to go home, I turn in the opposite direction and head over to his apartment.

His car is in the parking lot when I arrive, and I park in a visitor's space. *Wait, isn't he supposed to be at a business dinner?*

I fish his key out of my handbag and walk toward the door. Unlocking the door, I let myself into the living room. Immediately, I notice something is off—there's a shift in the air. Then I stumble, tripping over something.

"What the?" I mumble as I bend down to pick it up. Ethan keeps his place tidy. There shouldn't be anything on the floor. I hold up the item, and my whole body shudders in disgust as I realize it's a black lace bra. This is a shocking revelation. Not that this is a black lace bra, but the fact that it's not mine. The cups are too small to be mine. Someone else's black lace bra is on the floor of my fiancé's apartment.

His bedroom door opens, and out comes a woman. She turns on the lamp next to the coffee table, illuminating her appearance.

"Wait . . . Kristie?" I take a step forward.

She turns to face me. "Oh shit."

My hand goes up to silence her. I walk past her, storming into the bedroom. The brown eyes I always adored stare up at me—he's a deer caught in the headlights.

Without giving him a chance to speak, I go first.

"Ethan . . . what the fuck have you done to us?"

Acknowledgments

Chris: Thank you for supporting my crazy ideas. You're the green sauce to my red sauce, and I'll never throw you away.

Rachelle: Thank you for your kind words and edits. You've turned my draft into a story.

Dee: Thank you for proofreading! I love that I can depend on one last review and know you'll catch anything.

Gwen: Thanks for keeping me hyped up and pulling out all the stops for everything! You are my rockstar!

Pam: Glad you're not here for this one! I miss you. Love you to infinity and beyond.

And you. If you know me in real life—no. No, you don't.

More from Zoey Zane

Out Now

a beautiful broken life
He Calls Me Bug
(previously in Cheaters: A Dark Romance Anthology)
Countdown Madness

Coming Soon

Sweet Like Sugar, Thick Like Honey

Meet Zoey

Zoey Zane is an author and poet, but will always be a zealous reader at heart. She has a love for dark romance and thrillers, the two genres that dominate most of the space on her bookshelves. Zoey lives in Tennessee with her husband, their son, and their two adorable pit bulls.

You can find me at zoeyzane.net, by scanning the QR code, or on the sites below!

f facebook.com/zoeyzaneauthor

BB bookbub.com/authors/zoey-zane

g goodreads.com/author/show/20671544.Zoey_Zane

⊙ instagram.com/justmekendra/

a amazon.com/Zoey-Zane/e/B08K56BJZ2/

Made in the USA
Columbia, SC
06 August 2024